# ELVIS PRESLEY'S

## The First

# Noel

### ILLUSTRATED BY BRUCE WHATLEY

HARPERCOLLINSPUBLISHERS

*T*he first Noel

    the angel did say

Was to certain poor shepherds

    in fields as they lay.

In fields as they lay,

    keeping their sheep,

On a cold winter's night

    that was so deep.

*N*oel, Noel,

Noel, Noel,

Born is the king

of Israel.

They looked up
    and saw a star
Shining in the east
        beyond them far,
And to the earth
        it gave great light,
And so it continued
        both day and night.

Noel, Noel,
Noel, Noel,
Born is the king
of Israel.

*A*nd by the light

    of that same star

Three wise men came

    from country far;

To seek a king

    was their intent,

And to follow the star

    wherever it went.

*Noel, Noel,*

*Noel, Noel,*

*Born is the king*

*of Israel.*

*T*his star drew nigh

    to the northwest

O'er Bethlehem

    it took its rest,

And there it did

    both stop and stay

Right over the place

    where Jesus lay.

Noel, Noel,
Noel, Noel,
Born is the king
of Israel.

*Then* entered in

    those wise men three

Full reverently

    upon their knee,

And offered there

    in his presence

Their gold and myrrh

    and frankincense.

Noel, Noel,
Noel, Noel,
Born is the king
of Israel.

*To Michael, Jonathan,*
*Chris and Laura*
*Many thanks*
*—B.W.*

Elvis Presley's The First Noel

Arrangement and Adaptation by Elvis Presley

Copyright © 1971 (Renewed) by Elvis Presley Music

Elvis image, used by permission, © Elvis Presley Enterprises, Inc.

Illustrations copyright © 1999 by Bruce Whatley

Printed in China. All rights reserved. http://www.harperchildrens.com

LC Number: 99–71518

Typography by Al Cetta

1 2 3 4 5 6 7 8 9 10

❖

First Edition